# VALERIE'S NEW FRIENDS

## By Andrea D. Lewis, Ph.D.
### Illustrated by Al Danso

# Valerie's New Friends
## By Andrea D. Lewis, Ph.D.

RATHSI Publishing, LLC
rathsipublishing@gmail.com

ISBN: 978-1-936937-95-0

Andrea D. Lewis
alewis29@spelman.edu
(404) 270-5981

www.faculty.spelman.edu/andrealewis

Printed in The United States of America.

To Micah, Christian, and Alexander

Pelly-Marie,
Continue to shine in
God's light.
Andrea Terry

One hot summer day, Valerie watched a moving truck pull into the driveway of her new home. "I hope a girl my age lives nearby. We can play together and have sleepover parties," she said to her mother.

Valerie was eight years old. She had
sparkly brown eyes, two black curly
ponytails, and chocolate brown skin.
Valerie was excited to be moving into her
new home on Country Club Lane.

While the movers were unpacking the truck,
Valerie saw a girl across the street drawing
on the sidewalk and playing hopscotch.
Valerie was so happy to see a girl who
looked to be her age. She asked, "Mom, may
I go say hello?" After Valerie's mother said
yes, Valerie grabbed her bucket from the
driveway and ran across the street. She was
super excited!

"Hi, my name is Valerie. What's yours?",
asked Valerie. "My name is Maria, and I'm
eight years old," said the girl playing
hopscotch. "I'm eight, too!" exclaimed
Valerie. "Yeah! Grab a piece of chalk from
my bucket and let's draw!" said Valerie with
enthusiasm.

Maria was about the same size as Valerie. She had sparkly blue eyes and two blonde curly ponytails. There was a difference. Valerie was African American and Maria was Caucasian.

Although Maria had never played with an African American child before, she remembered hearing her parents say that it was fun to meet children from different backgrounds. Her parents and grandparents taught her that everyone does not have to look the same to play together. In fact, Maria's grandparents had marched alongside African Americans in the 1960s during the Civil Rights Movement.

Valerie and Maria became best friends over the summer. They had tea parties, walked to the library, and went swimming. One day during a trip to the shopping mall, they each bought a Best Friends Forever bracelet. Valerie's bracelet had a gold heart with Maria's name engraved on it and Maria's bracelet had a gold heart with Valerie's name engraved on it.

When the first day of school arrived, Valerie and Maria waited anxiously for the school bus and sat together as they hopped into their seats. "I'm so excited about meeting my new teacher," said Valerie!"

The girls continued to talk and giggle about their hopes for the school day. All of a sudden the girl's laughter was interrupted by the sound of hissing and name calling. As they looked around, they saw some of the other children on the bus pointing at Valerie and calling her names because of her chocolate brown skin. They laughed at Valerie as they called her bad names. Hurt and upset by their comments, Valerie cried. Marie shouted at the other children and told them that they were being rude. Maria held Valerie's hand and tried to comfort her. Once the bus arrived at school, Maria led Valerie to the principal's office.

OFFICE

Valerie was very unhappy. "Why don't the other children like me?", she thought to herself. Then she realized that she was the only African American child in her neighborhood. Valerie sat quietly in the school office and tried not to cry. She really wished that her parents would pick her up from school. She never wanted to return again.

The principal, Mrs. Marion, was quite upset to hear that the students on the bus were mean to Valerie. Mrs. Marion told Valerie that she was welcome at Wilson Elementary School. The principal spoke to Valerie's classmates and shared her sadness at their actions. She reminded them to never judge people by the color of their skin, but rather by how they treat you.

The next day when Valerie got off of the school bus, some of the children began teasing her. Valerie said, "Sticks and stones may break my bones, but names will never hurt me." The children picked up sticks and stones and threw them at Valerie!

The truth was that the words hurt more than the sticks and stones. The words stung and left a lasting hurt inside Valerie's heart. Valerie did not throw sticks back at the children, nor did she cry. Valerie remembered what her parents told her. "Keep your head up and remember who you are." She also remembered that her grandparents had been courageous and had fought for freedom and civil rights. They had marched in the Civil Rights Movement to make sure African Americans had equal rights in America. Her grandfather had attended the March on Washington in 1963 and had participated in sit-ins. Valerie became stronger as she remembered these things. She looked straight at the children and did not blink her eyes.

When Valerie did not cry, the children stopped throwing sticks at her. They saw that Valerie was strong and believed in herself.

When Valerie got home, she ran to her room and cried. At dinnertime, she told her parents what happened when she got off the school bus. Valerie's mother and father were proud of her for remembering to be courageous and strong. Valerie's parents gave her a big hug. After dinner, Valerie's father quietly left the house.

Valerie's father went to the homes of the children who teased his daughter. He spoke to their parents and shared his disappointment at their children's words and actions. The parents were surprised and saddened that their children threw sticks and stones at Valerie. The parents promised that it would not happen again.

After many weeks, the students began to get to
know Valerie. They realized she was not that
different after all. Valerie earned good grades,
enjoyed the same activities as the other
children, and was always kind to everyone.
Valerie was invited to play at her new friends'
homes and to their birthday parties. Valerie
was happy to be included in her new friends'
lives.

The principal, Mrs. Marion, invited Valerie to participate in a special assembly program on differences. Valerie greeted her new friends, "Although we may look different, we can all learn from each other and learn to get along with each other. It only takes an open mind and a loving heart."

Valerie and her new friends learned that differences make the world a better place.

# Valerie's New Friends Teaching Guide

Parents and Educators,

Valerie's New Friends is the story of my childhood that I wanted to share, especially with children who experience schooling in the same manner as I did. Attending school as the different child in the class and community was not a pleasant experience. School was not a place of comfort or nurturing.

Valerie's New Friends speaks to racial acceptance, but the message translates to concepts of difference and diversity. Given the increasing diversity of schools and communities in the 21st century, children need to be taught how to accept others and make every child feel welcomed into their community of learners.

As schools create inclusive learning environments, it is vitally important that educators value and embrace diverse viewpoints, recognize their own personal biases, and most importantly, promote diversity awareness among teachers, parents, and students in schools. Diversity efforts include everyone and exclude no one.

In allowing children to recognize differences, it is important to teach children proper terminology to describe others. Children are capable of understanding and using non-offensive and non-threatening describing words. Additionally, learning environments must be inclusive of multicultural ways of implementing varying perspectives and styles of educating diverse children in each classroom. A strong learning community is one that honors, supports, and challenges each learner to be a uniquely contributing member.

It is my hope that you will find this book not only helpful, but a positive approach to celebrating and confronting differences among children.

Touching the future,

*Andrea D. Lewis, PhD*

# Lesson Plan for Valerie's New Friends
## Created by: Andrea D. Lewis, Ph.D.

Objective:
Students will recognize, understand, and respect differences and diversity in their classroom, school, and community.

Materials:
Valerie's New Friends; chart paper - one with a large elephant in center; markers; sticky notes; shoebox decorated with elephants

Opening:
Write the word 'diversity' on the board. Ask students to provide short definitions of the term. Record the student responses on an anchor chart. After the discussion, read Valerie's New Friends.

Activity:
Draw a large elephant on chart paper. Ask students if they know the meaning of the phrase "elephant in the room". The phrase refers to a difficult problem that people do not want to discuss. If students have been introduced to idioms, the teacher can extend the lesson to include meanings and uses of idioms. After examining the phrase, refer back to the diversity anchor chart. Explain that differences can be difficult to discuss, but like the children in Valerie's New Friends, children can work together to embrace and learn from differences. Discuss various types of differences (racial, ethnic, gender, religious, age, language, sexual orientation, social class, ableism, regional, etc.). This list can be shortened or expanded based upon the grade level of the students. Have a conversation about differences and allow children to share personal stories, if desired.

Explain that disrespect for differences will not be tolerated in the classroom. Open dialogue and sharing will be permitted, as well as the teaching of non-derogatory terms. Based on the grade level of the students, examples of positive and derogatory terminology can be considered.

Give each student a sticky note and instruct the class to write a word or phrase on their sticky note that describes why differences should be embraced. Model examples include "to empower others", "to work together", and "to share feelings".

Diversity and difference are ongoing and complex concepts that cannot be confined to a singular lesson. Explain to students that the conversation is an introduction to diversity and follow up activities will take place on a consistent basis.

Assessment options:
1. Ask students to recall phrases/incidents from Valerie's New Friends. In two columns, have students write or type the phrase/incident in one column and their refection in the second column. The reflection should include students' thoughts on whether or not they could relate to the phrase/incident.
2. Create a poem, song, or movie related to diversity and differences.
3. Assign a follow up book to read and complete a comprehension project.
4. Design a technological project describing the importance of celebrating differences.

## Ongoing Follow Up Activity:

Post the completed elephant chart on the wall or bulletin board in the class, along with an elephant question box. When students have a question about differences and diversity in the class or community, they can write the question or comment in the elephant box anonymously. During each class meeting, the teacher will devote time on the agenda for a diversity talk to discuss students' questions, comments, or concerns located in the elephant box.

# Lesson Plans for the Civil Rights Movement
## Created by: Andrea D. Lewis, Ph.D.

In Valerie's New Friends, both Valerie and Maria's grandparents participated in the Civil Rights Movement of the 1950s and 1960s in America. The following activities may be used to teach students about this time period.

## Take a Walk in My Shoes

All journeys begin with a single footstep. The Civil Rights Movement was successful because brave individuals put a foot forward and worked for equality. On September 14, 2004, a permanent exhibit which showcases the footprints of important civil rights advocates was unveiled at the Martin Luther King, Jr. National Historic Site in Atlanta, Georgia. The International Civil Rights Walk of Fame has the cemented footprints of Ralph David Abernathy, President Jimmy Carter, Thurgood Marshall, Medgar Evers, Rosa Parks, and many more. Six hundred spaces are reserved for current and future footprints.

Your team has been assigned to create an International Civil Rights Walk of Fame at your school. Using butcher paper, construction paper, and markers, construct a replica of this display. Create and label shoes of famous men and women who participated in the Civil Rights Movement. Include individuals who have not been featured in the current International Walk of Fame.

In your group, discuss why you chose each individual and why their contributions were significant. Your presentation should include your task, summary of your discussion, and viewing of your final project.

## Back to The Future

In the 1980s, a popular movie series featured Marty McFly, a typical American teenager, who was sent into the past in a plutonium-powered time machine invented by a mad scientist.

Your group is traveling in a time machine back to the Civil Rights era. Design an original time machine and choose an event or place to visit from the days of the Civil Rights Movement. In your team illustrate your time machine, the reason for selecting your destination, what you will do when you arrive, and if your participation in the event will leave a lasting legacy.

Your presentation should include your task, replica of your time machine, picture and description of your destination, and summary of your group discussion.

# Oral History Project

According to the Oral History Association, "oral history is a method of gathering and preserving historical information through recorded interviews of people about past events and ways of life."

Your team has been awarded a grant from the Oral History Association to highlight famous Americans from the Civil Rights Movement. Select a civil rights activist and create a fictional oral history interview based on published facts in literature. Create a written interview using your own questions and answer them in the way you believe the interviewee might have answered. Although the answers should be based on published facts about the civil rights activist, you are encouraged to use creativity when developing responses.

In your team discuss who you will choose to interview, the reason for your selection, the setting of your interview and at least 7 thought-provoking questions and answers. Your presentation should include your task, summary of your group discussion, and reenactment of your oral history with your historical figure and interviewer.

# Civil Rights Tour

Your team has been selected to plan a Spring Break Civil Rights Tour departing from your hometown. Select at least five historical sites on your tour that are located in three different cities. Using destinations mentioned in Civil Rights literature, create a realistic and meaningful trip for your classmates.

In your team discuss your destinations, the reason for selecting the historical sites, what you hope your classmates will gain from the experience, and a budget.

Your presentation should include your task, highlights from a parent orientation to include the cost and destinations, and summary of your group discussion.

CPSIA information can be obtained at www.ICGtesting.com
Printed in the USA
LVIW01n0726260417
532018LV00001B/6